WIN A JINN

GET YOUR WISHES FULFILLED

OMER DAVID

Made with ♥ on the Notion Press Platform
www.notionpress.com

Contents

CHAPTER 1

The Promise

In the big story of human history and myths, few parts are as closely connected as the Jinn. These mysterious beings have been talked about in stories across different cultures and places, stories that have lasted a really long time. But what if these stories were more than just made-up? What if the Jinn were real, not just something people imagined, and their power could be found by those brave enough to look for it?

You all heard the story of the Jinn grant your wishes, you may wish for that Jinn to appear in your life. I am here to tell you that it's not just a folk tale. I can promise you that the existence of jinns are real and you can master them. It's not an easy process but it's possible. No one really knows about these mythical creatures except the stories passed through generations. Are you ready to take on this power? Get ready to explore the fascinating world of jinn with me as your guide. I promise you, jinns are real.

The barrier between our world and the mystical one is delicate, like a thin piece of fabric that moves with even a gentle touch. On the other side of this barrier is a place where Jinn live, and their presence is like a dance of light and shadow. In this place, wishes, wants, and thoughts shape how things happen, creating the way things are. The Jinn's power is like a channel and a force that makes things change in this special realm.

To understand and use the Jinn's power in this special place, you need to realize that what we think is real is just a small part of everything. Science tries to uncover the secrets of the universe, but it can't explain everything, especially the things that are about the spirit or mind. Like how tiny particles move in a certain way, our thoughts and awareness might also have a connection to things we can't see.

Think about what old wise people said long ago, like those who talked about energies and forces we can't feel. The Jinn represent these hidden energies. To truly get them, we have to know that the universe is way more complex than we can understand with our basic senses. We have to know that inside us, there's a chance to connect with these energies, to be in tune with how everything works together.

You might wonder why we don't know much about Jinn. It's because they exist in a way that's hard for us to grasp. They live in places we can't really understand using our usual ideas. Their reality is like a mix of different vibes, kind of like a pattern made of vibrations. To notice them, we have to change how we think and be okay with not having easy answers.

Now, let's talk about getting really good at understanding Jinn. It's not something you can do if you're not very serious about it. You have to be fully committed and really work to understand yourself and how everything fits together. This journey asks us to dig deep into our wants, fears, and thoughts. Jinn aren't just there to make wishes come true – they show us who we are and what we could be.

Imagine you're at the entrance of a secret garden, where every flower represents a part of who you are. To become good at handling Jinn is like taking care of this garden. You help the good parts grow strong and get rid of the bad parts. You make your thoughts clear and strong, like an artist shaping something with a tool. By meditating and thinking about yourself, you get in tune with where the Jinn are.

What I'm saying isn't about getting what you want right away, but about finding something really important. I'm here to give you advice from old wisdom and new knowledge. It's like bringing together things that are magical and things that work in real life. I've learned how to understand Jinn, and now I'm offering to help you. This journey won't be easy, though. It's like a trip to learn a lot about yourself and connect with something big in the universe.

The impact of Jinns is evident across diverse cultures globally, spanning various religions and their sacred texts. Jinn, though recognized by that name, also go by different names in different contexts. They have left their mark in stories and beliefs from various parts of the world.

In Islamic and Arabian stories, Jinn are special creatures made by God from "smokeless fire." They're talked about in the Quran and Hadiths, which are sayings of Prophet Muhammad. Jinn have their own societies, skills, and choices. They can be good, bad, or just in between, and they do things with people in different ways. People think Jinn can do powerful things like change shape, disappear, take over, and make wishes come true.

In Persian stories, Jinn are known as "Divs" or "Deevs." They're often linked with wild places and confusion. People show them as strong, sometimes not nice creatures, but like in Arabian tales, they can also be good or just okay.

In stories from South Asia, Jinn are called "Jinnat." People believe they live in places without people, like old buildings or caves, and can change what happens to people. Jinn can be helpful or harmful, and there are ways to stay safe from their power.

In other parts of the world, like Japan and Burma, there are similar ideas about strong beings that do things like Jinn. In Japan, they're called "Youkai," and in Burma, they're "Nat."

Throughout history and even in the present day, many individuals have been connected to Jinns, seeking their assistance for personal growth and progress. Now, it's your opportunity to enhance your life and make significant advancements with their help. You can choose to just watch normal things happen, or you can join in and be a part of everything. I promise you'll discover new things, change, and become stronger. Jinn are real, and you can understand their power. As you walk this path, let your reason guide you, your curiosity keep you interested, and your spirit be full of hope and chances. As you start on this journey, remember that you're not alone.

I promised that the existence of Jinns is real, and if you follow this journey through my guidance, you can win a Jinn. I also promise that I'm simplifying the process as much as possible. I don't want to confuse you with unnecessary details or complexities, so I'm keeping everything minimal and straightforward for you.

CHAPTER 2

The Others

In this cosmic tale, humans, angels, demons, and Jinn are all considered children of a higher power, part of something divine. But how they interact with each other remains a big puzzle. Jinn, especially, are confusing. They're neither all good nor all bad; some follow angels, others go with demons, and some remain neutral. Humans, however, are seen as complex. We can be very kind or terribly cruel, incredibly creative or horribly destructive. We have something unique: free will. This means we can make choices, leading to endless possibilities but also heavy consequences. In this shared story of creation, all these entities coexist. Angels glow with heavenly light, demons blaze with fiery intensity, Jinn are wrapped in a smoky mystery, and humans, well, we're made from the Earth, a blend of clay and spirit. Each one has something special, all contributing to the universe's balance. humans find themselves in a unique spot. Some see us as lucky, while others view us as cursed. But consider this: could we be the ones being tricked, living in a massive game created by powers we can't understand?

humans truly dive deep into emotions, from love to anger, from joy to sadness. We grapple with right and wrong, good and evil. While angels, demons, and Jinn often stick to their nature, we humans have the power to choose and shape our lives. In this grand creation tale, humans, sometimes called the fooled ones, possess a wisdom beyond just being made from clay. We explore, question, and seek understanding even when things are uncertain. We find meaning in our sometimes chaotic lives. And as we search for knowledge and truth, we unravel the mysteries of our existence, shedding light on the universe's great design.

In the big picture of supernatural beings, humans have something truly special: the ability to make choices. While creatures like Jinns, angels, and demons might be bound by their nature or duties to higher powers, humans can decide their own paths. This power sets them apart.This freedom lets humans aim for greatness. They can explore different paths, follow their passions, and dream big. Every choice they make not only shapes their own future but also impacts the world around them.But what makes this power even more amazing is that many people don't realize its full potential. Lots of humans go through life without understanding just how strong they are inside. This hidden strength remains one of humanity's biggest mysteries.Imagine if everyone knew the power they had. They could not only change their own lives but also make the world a better place. Every decision, every dream could create positive change. People could overcome challenges, challenge unfair rules, and build a world full of kindness and understanding. In the grand scheme of things, humans have this incredible gift—the power to shape their own destinies,

In the world of supernatural beings, angels are often seen as really special. People think they're closest to the creator or the big divine power. They have some serious powers, but they don't use them like superheroes to help others. Angels have a different job – they're like cosmic messengers and keepers of the divine plan. They use their powers mainly to keep things in balance when something goes really wrong in the universe. One of their main gigs is to make sure everything in the universe stays in order. They have to keep the peace and stop any troublemakers, including Jinns, from messing things up. It's like they're the cosmic referees, making sure everyone plays by the rules.

But here's the thing: angels aren't always perfect. Just like humans and Jinns, they can be good or bad, kind or strict. Some stories even say there have been times when angels rebelled against their boss, the big divine power. So, they're not always the picture of pure goodness. In short, angels are important in many belief systems, but they're not as simple as they might seem. Their relationships with humans and Jinns are way more complex than just being good guys.

In many belief systems, there's a common idea of demons going against angels and the divine rules. It's kind of like when someone speaks out against their government and gets labeled as a troublemaker. In this case, demons are the ones who rebel against angels and, in a bigger way, the creator or the higher power. The thought of a being changing from being an angel to becoming a demon is pretty interesting. It suggests that angels, who are usually seen as obedient and never questioning things, can also have their own thoughts and doubts. Some stories say the first demon was actually an angel who dared to think for themselves and speak out against unfairness. This bold move led to a big change, and that's when the first demon came to be.

After this first act of rebellion, more and more beings became demons. Some of them used to be angels, while others might have been Jinns or even humans who did really bad things. The word "demon" is often used for those who do mean and harmful things or challenge the usual order of things, either because they choose to or because someone higher up forces them to.The change from being full of light (angelic) to fiery (demonic) represents a big shift in their nature and what they're all about. Demons are often shown as beings of chaos, rebellion, and causing destruction. People are usually scared of them and sometimes even really don't like them because of what they do, which goes against how things are supposed to be.

The stories about demons standing up against what's unfair and not right show a bigger idea. They remind us that even when there's someone or something really powerful in charge, there's still a chance for regular folks or beings to speak up, question things, and fight for what they believe is fair. Even though demons often get a bad rap, their stories tell us that the human (and supernatural) spirit can keep pushing against unfairness and injustice, even if it means going down a tougher path.

Some people have discovered these hidden secrets among humans, and they've made these mysteries a part of their lives. This has elevated them beyond being labeled as "the fooled ones." They've delved deeper into the world of the supernatural and learned to use its power. Now, why many humans seem to have forgotten these truths is quite interesting. One idea is that humans possess a special power, even though they might not be aware of it. This power sets them apart from supernatural beings like Jinns, angels, and demons. In certain philosophical beliefs, it's thought that the most powerful force controlling the universe could be a human-like being. This being would have the incredible ability to shape reality as they want, essentially having the power to do anything they desire.

This idea challenges the usual belief that humans are weaker or less powerful in the hierarchy of supernatural beings. Instead, it suggests that humans, with their free will and untapped potential, might have the ability to compete with or even outdo other entities in the grand cosmic story. making us think about our own abilities and the mysteries within the human experience. It suggests that humans could hold the answers to the biggest secrets of the universe, including the nature of our existence. Human with power is God

Humans possess an incredible power that often goes unnoticed - the ability to control Jinns. This knowledge is deeply rooted in ancient wisdom, like a secret cheat code for life. Many humans have forgotten this truth, believing they're bound by life's rules. But in reality, Jinns, these mysterious and powerful beings, aren't beyond human control; in fact, they seek humans as masters or friends. This unique advantage is like a hidden tool in human life. It's not about enslaving Jinns; it's more of a partnership, where both sides benefit. The idea of getting help from Jinns isn't new; throughout history, people have used this assistance. They haven't faced life's challenges alone; Jinns have played a role in their successes, a fact that often goes unnoticed.

You might think it sounds unbelievable - the idea that humans can shape their destinities with the help of Jinns. But this partnership isn't forced; it's a choice. Jinns are willing allies; they want to help humans. They're not acting against their own will; they genuinely desire this connection.This ancient understanding challenges the usual way we see things, reminding humanity that they're not helpless when facing life's difficulties. This isn't cheating; it's an innate ability, a gift from the universe. It's a reminder that humans aren't alone on their life's journey; they have powerful allies waiting to assist them.

Throughout history, many remarkable people have left a lasting impact on the world. Some of their incredible achievements may have had a mysterious ingredient: the help of Jinns. While not every great accomplishment can be attributed to this supernatural collaboration, there are many instances where it seems to have played a role.Think about scientific discoveries. Sometimes, scientists and inventors have sudden moments of genius that lead to groundbreaking findings. These "eureka" moments are crucial for human progress. While we don't know where these insights come from, the idea that Jinns might be involved is fascinating.

The world of art and creativity has also seen incredible transformations. Some people who were once seen as ordinary suddenly become legendary artists. Their talent seems to come out of nowhere, captivating people and leaving a lasting legacy. In these cases, it's possible that

Jinns subtly guided their creative process, taking them from ordinary to extraordinary. Even in the history of wars and conquests, there are moments where unexpected events or interventions changed the course of history. Battles that seemed lost were suddenly won, and fortunes shifted dramatically. These unexplainable events make you wonder if supernatural forces, like Jinns, were at play.

It's important to note that acknowledging the influence of Jinns in these remarkable achievements doesn't take away from the hard work and talent of individuals. Instead, it highlights the idea that greatness often comes from collaboration, even if we don't fully understand how it works. The involvement of Jinns, if it exists, reminds us that our world is interconnected, where human ambition and mysterious forces can come together to create extraordinary results.It reminds us that greatness isn't always a solo journey; sometimes, partnerships, even with supernatural beings, can lead to incredible outcomes.

The idea might seem like something out of a fantasy story, but it holds a truth that's been known for ages. Embracing this partnership isn't about taking shortcuts; it's about recognizing that everything in the universe is connected. Humans and Jinns, even though different, can come together to create a reality that goes beyond what seems possible.This knowledge isn't just an old tale; it's a living truth that's waiting to be rediscovered. By understanding this alliance, humans can open doors to possibilities beyond their wildest dreams. It's a reminder that humans are the masters of their own destinies, not just pieces moved around in life's game. This 'cheat code' isn't about finding an easy way out; it's about using the incredible potential that lies within, a potential that, when combined with the help of Jinns, can lead to remarkable achievements.

In this book, I'm only talking about how people can connect with Jinns and do amazing things in life. I want to stress that humans have a lot of untapped potential, and what I am going to cover here is just the start. I'll go into greater detail in the next parts of this book. So. Keep reading to find out more about how humans and jinns can work together to achieve incredible things.

CHAPTER 3

Jinns

In the wide world of religious beliefs and stories, some creatures stand out as incredibly intriguing and puzzling, and one of these is the Jinn. When it comes to understanding Jinn, Islam has a particularly rich tradition. Over many centuries, the sacred texts of this religion and the scholars who study them have created a web of information and fascination around these mystical beings. In Islam, Jinn are very important. They have intrigued people for a long time and are often shown as mysterious, not-of-this-world creatures who live on the edges of our reality. The Quran, the holy book of Islam, talks about Jinn multiple times, showing that they have a significant place in the religion's stories and beliefs.

According to Islamic teachings, one interesting thing about Jinn is how long they live. They are believed to have a lifespan of thousands of years, much longer than humans. Different stories mention different lengths, but some say Jinn can live for 5,000 to 8,000 years, or even longer. This really makes them different from us, as they exist in a kind of time that's unlike ours. What's even more interesting is that Jinn were here before humans. It means they've been on Earth longer than we have, this means they have a very long history, where they watched the world change over time.

Nobody really knows how many Jinn there are. It's a big mystery, and we can only guess. But it's sure there are way more Jinn than humans. because Jinn live for such a long time, and they've been around longer than us. But we can't say for sure how many of them there are. It's a secret, just like the Jinn themselves. They live in a world that's very different from ours. We can't really understand how they exist or the rules they follow. Their way of life is a mystery to us, making them even more intriguing and puzzling.

Jinns live in their own world, which is close to our own, but they prefer to stay hidden. They are not interested in bothering us, and they mostly like to watch us from afar. This sets them apart from other supernatural creatures in stories from different cultures, which often interact with humans in more direct and sometimes not-so-friendly ways. Jinn are like shy neighbors who live next door but never come out to say hello. They are curious about us, but they don't want to get involved in our lives. Jinn have various reasons for choosing to stay away from us. Jinn stay away from humans for a few reasons. First, they're very different from us, so it's hard for them to connect.

Second, they live much longer than us, so our short lives might not matter much to them. They also respect our freedom and don't want to mess with it. And maybe there's a rule from a higher power that stops them from getting involved in human matters.

Jinns, these fascinating beings, live with us, but we can't see, hear, or feel them. Some are in different dimensions, and some are right here, beside us. The strange thing is, we can't sense them at all—they're like shadows, existing in a way that our usual senses can't grasp .Our eyes, which can see colors and shapes, can't catch a glimpse of these mysterious creatures. Our ears, tuned to sounds, can't pick up any noises they might make. Our senses, designed to feel the world, can't detect them in any manner. It's like they're in a place our senses can't reach. Surprisingly, we do have the ability to see Jinn, but it's like a hidden power within us, inactive and undiscovered. However, it's actually a good thing that we can't perceive them. These Jinn share our spaces, our homes, and the places we go. It's even possible that where you live, Jinn might be there too. Essentially, we might be living in their world without even knowing it.

Humans and Jinn are incredibly diverse beings, each with their unique backgrounds and beliefs. Just as humans belong to different cultures, Jinn also carry their own cultural heritage and traditions. These differences create a complex mosaic, showing the intricacies of life for both humans and Jinn.Just like humans can be kind, compassionate, or mischievous, Jinn also have a wide range of personalities. Some Jinn are helpful and protective, while others might be playful or curious. This variety adds depth to the Jinn world, making them similar to the diverse human personalities we encounter.Both humans and Jinn experience a range of emotions, including love, joy, anger, and sadness. These universal feelings connect us on a deep level. Jinn, like humans, form strong emotional bonds and navigate the complexities of relationships. This shared emotional capacity highlights that Jinn, despite their supernatural origin, experience similar profound emotions that make life meaningful.

Additionally, just as humans have their societies with leaders and social structures, Jinn also form communities with intricate dynamics. They have relationships, alliances, and conflicts, mirroring the complexities of human interactions.This similarity between humans and Jinn shows how interconnected all beings are, regardless of where they come from. It underscores the shared qualities that tie us together, reminding us that beneath our differences, we all share a common existence.

Jinns have different powers. Some can do anything, like granting wishes and performing amazing feats. Others are only experts at hiding from humans, staying unnoticed. When asking for help, it's essential to match your needs with a Jinn's abilities. Some are good at healing or providing guidance, while others influence love or wealth. By choosing the right Jinn for your specific goal, you increase the chances of a successful partnership.Understanding what each Jinn can do is like knowing a group of experts. It's like having a team with different specialties. So, when asking for help from a Jinn, it's important to know what you need. Find the Jinn whose abilities match your goals. This way, your expectations will be realistic, and your collaboration with them will have a better chance of success. Jinns offer a world of possibilities with their diverse powers. Understanding and respecting their abilities can help you achieve a variety of desires and goals. So, when dealing with Jinns, it's not just about believing but also about making wise and well-informed choices.

out of the many Jinn types, we're focusing on these nine types of Jinns because they are significant and have diverse powers. Even within these nine types, there are many variations. What's interesting is that a Jinn's abilities can change over time. They're not stuck with the powers they're born with; they can grow and become stronger based on what they do and experience in life. Each of these nine types has its own unique traits. Some might be strong from the beginning, while others might be considered weaker. But what makes Jinns special is that they can become more powerful as they live their lives.

It's crucial to understand that a Jinn's powers can change. They can get better at what they do through their actions and the things they go through. This means their strength isn't just determined by how they were born but also by the choices they make and the paths they take. The Jinns can evolve and become more powerful Knowing about these nine types of Jinns can help you get what you want. Even if some of them are seen as not very strong at first, remember that they can become more powerful over time. This means you don't always have to look for the strongest Jinn; even the ones considered less strong can assist you effectively. The important thing is to understand what each type can do and how they can grow and then choose the one that matches your desires to make your wishes come true.

Marid

The Marid is a particular type of Jinn known for its immense power and unique characteristics. The power of Marids is truly unimaginable Among the various classes of Jinns, Marids are often regarded as the most powerful and influential, their abilities as almost limitless they possess immense power and authority. Marids are capable of doing extraordinary things that go beyond what humans can understand. Their capabilities are often described as near-omnipotent

Marids are strongly linked to water, a symbol of life and purity in various cultures. Water represents sustenance and vitality for all living beings. Marids embody this life-giving essence, similar to how water is essential for life on Earth. They are seen as vital and potent beings among the world of Jinns. They are sometimes referred to as "water spirits" or "sea Jinns."

The Marids possess incredible power, allowing them to accomplish nearly anything, making them highly desired by those seeking supernatural help. However, controlling a Marid is incredibly difficult due to their independent and resistant nature. They do not easily obey commands, making it very difficult to harness their abilities.

Connecting with Marids is tough, and controlling them is even harder. But even a small connection can be hugely beneficial. It can give you access to valuable knowledge and skills. Although it's hard, the things you can learn and do through this connection can change your life. So, even if it's challenging, trying to form a bond with a Marid is definitely worth it.

I wouldn't suggest trying to connect with Marids when you're just starting out. It's a tough journey that takes a lot of time and hard work. It's like trying to climb the tallest mountain, which can seem really challenging at first. However, the rewards and outcomes you can achieve through this connection are incredible and beyond what you can even imagine. So, it's something to think about once you've gained more knowledge and experience with Jinns. Remember, there are other types of Jinns that might be easier for beginners to connect with.

Ifrit

Ifrits are known for their exceptional intelligence and cleverness. They have an incredible ability to find solutions to various problems and discover hidden secrets. Among supernatural beings, Ifrits are renowned for their deep knowledge of the universe's mysteries. They are often seen as wise beings who hold answers to even the most puzzling questions. Their skill in navigating complex situations and offering insights into complicated matters makes them highly desired.

Their intelligence isn't limited to just knowing things; it also includes their ability to think strategically and make wise decisions. They can quickly and accurately analyze situations, coming up with precise plans and solutions. This strategic thinking adds to their reputation as highly intelligent beings in the supernatural world. Their sharp minds and clever nature allow them to explore the depths of knowledge, revealing secrets and providing insights that are beyond most people's understanding.

Ifrits are connected to fire, which reflects their fiery and intense personality. Like fire, they have a strong and sometimes hard-to-control anger that can be both powerful and difficult to manage. Interacting with Ifrits can be challenging because of their hot-headed and fierce nature. Their anger is like blazing flames, showing their untamed energy and strong abilities. This passionate nature can make dealing with them unpredictable and potentially explosive. To approach an Ifrit safely, you must be cautious and show them the utmost respect, as their fiery temper requires careful handling to avoid making them very angry.

Ifrits mirror the qualities of fire, fierce and hard to predict. Their anger can make them stronger or cause trouble, just like fire can bring warmth or destruction. To deal with them, you need patience, understanding, and respect for their fiery nature. They're often seen as bad, but they can also be loyal, brave, and loving. However, if you don't handle their incredible power and fiery temper carefully, it can lead to chaos.

Silat

Silat Jinns, also known as shapeshifter Jinns, have an amazing ability to change into anything they want, be it humans, animals, or objects. They don't seem to have any limits to their shapeshifting skills, and they can stay in these forms for as long as they like. What makes them fascinating is that they can live among humans, taking on human forms effortlessly. They blend in so well that it's hard to tell who they really are. This skill allows them to form deep connections with humans, even having relationships and children with them. When Silat Jinns have children with humans, these children inherit qualities from both worlds. They might have supernatural abilities while living as part of the human society.

Silat Jinns are indeed around us, and sometimes their presence is more apparent than we realize. However, it's important to know that these Jinns usually don't have superpowers to directly help you They prefer to stay hidden and not attract attention. As you progress in your journey, you might discover that someone you've known or met is actually a Silat Jinn. In such cases, it's vital to be careful and use caution. Approaching them directly and asking about their true identity can lead to negative outcomes. It's better to be patient and show restraint. If a Silat Jinn wants to reveal their true nature to you, they will do it in their own time and in their own way. Forcing them to disclose their identity prematurely can harm your relationship and have adverse effects.

To connect with silat Jinns, trust is crucial. They naturally want to help, and if they see you as honest and reliable, they might reveal themselves and assist you when they're ready. Rushing or pressuring them won't work. Instead, focus on being trustworthy. Eventually, they may come forward to offer guidance and support you. Being patient and sincere is key to connecting with these mysterious beings.

Jann

Jann Jinns are different from other supernatural beings because they are usually friendly towards humans. They are known for helping and interacting with people in a positive manner. They are happy to help and engage with us. This friendliness is special because in the world of Jinns, where many beings can be tricky or even mean, Janns are kind and easy to approach. Janns are also very peaceful and value good friendships a lot.

Jann Jinns are strongly connected to the element of earth. They deeply cherish nature and are known as its protectors. But it's not just the environment they guard; they also protect all the living creatures that call it home. Their link with nature isn't just about a deep appreciation; it gives them extraordinary power. This power makes them the unwavering guardians of our planet's wonders. Their role is crucial in maintaining the delicate balance of the natural world.These beings represent the intricate connection between the supernatural and nature's beauty. They are like the watchful caretakers of the Earth. Their purpose is to ensure that the world's splendor endures for generations to come.

Jann Jinns are special beings that live in many different places, like deserts, forests, and mountains. They're like guardians of these places, and they have a very important job: helping people when they're in trouble.Think about this: you're lost in a huge desert or a thick forest. It's a scary situation because there's no one around to help you. But suddenly, out of nowhere, a stranger appears. They seem to know the desert or forest like the back of their hand. They guide you, showing you the way to safety and providing you with the knowledge you need to survive.

These moments have happened to some of you, and you've probably wondered about that mysterious stranger. Janns come to your aid when you're at your most vulnerable, lost and alone in the wilderness. Their help is often crucial, as the advice they give can mean the difference between life and death in tough terrains. Their deep bond with nature gives them a special understanding of these places. They guide you back, ensuring not just survival but also valuable lessons from the experience.

These moments can be life-saving because the advice and guidance they provide can mean the difference between life and death in tough environments. Their deep connection to nature gives them a unique understanding of these terrains. They help you find your way back, ensuring you not only survive but also learn from the experience. In these remote and harsh locations, Jann Jinns act as saviors, like guiding lights that appear when you need them the most. After helping, they usually disappear just as mysteriously as they arrived, leaving behind a strong feeling of gratitude and amazement.

At least once in a lifetime, nearly everyone encounters a Jann, a mystical being that appears just when hope is fading or disaster is about to strike. It could be a time when you've lost all hope, or when a terrible event is prevented by a seemingly small action. During these crucial moments, the help of a Jann can make all the difference. Their presence is more than just assistance; it's a significant moment, a time when destiny shifts, and life unexpectedly takes a positive turn

Nasnas

Nasnas Jinns are a unique kind of Jinns. They have a special ability: they can look like animals. These Jinns are not super powerful, and they are usually harmless. They're known for being playful and friendly, often hanging out with humans and other animals. What's really interesting about Nasnas Jinns is that they're kind of like half-human, half-animal. Unlike some other Jinns who can completely turn into humans, Nasnas Jinns can't do that. Instead, they can copy the looks and behaviors of animals. So, they're sort of in-between, not fully human and not fully animal.

This in-between state lets them fit into both the human world and the animal world. They're pretty flexible and can adapt to different situations. Even though they don't have superpowers like some other Jinns, Nasnas Jinns make up for it with their friendly and loving nature. People usually enjoy their company because they bring happiness and fun wherever they go. Instead of being scary, they're seen as wonderful companions.

Nasnas Jinns often like to appear as household pets, especially cats. They love human attention and affection, especially when they take the form of these beloved animals. As cats, Nasnas enjoy being cuddled and played with by people. They are playful and charming, making them treasured companions. Those who have Nasnas cats in their homes find joy and happiness in their presence. These cats form strong connections with their human friends, bringing a sense of warmth and companionship to the households they live in. Their playful and loving nature adds a magical touch to everyday life, making them not just pets but beloved family members.

Palis

Palis Jinns are incredibly ancient and mysterious beings. They live in the shadows, making it nearly impossible for even other Jinns to find them. Just the mention of their name excites and intrigues supernatural beings everywhere. Why? Because Palis Jinns are known as the protectors of ancient treasures, but not the kind you might expect. When we think of treasures, we usually picture gold, jewels, and precious gems. But the treasures guarded by Palis Jinns are much more profound. They protect knowledge and power, items that hold secrets about the universe, life, and existence itself. Imagine ancient scrolls filled with wisdom from centuries ago or magical artifacts with abilities that humans can't even imagine. These are the treasures Palis Jinns watch over.

Palis Jinns have a vital role as protectors that goes way beyond guarding physical items. They watch over ancient wisdom, forgotten civilizations, and mystical knowledge. Their duty is to make sure that the wisdom of our ancestors remains safe over time. But here's the thing, they don't share this precious knowledge with just anyone. They only reveal their secrets to those they think are deserving.

Meeting a Palis Jinn is extremely rare and significant. If you happen to encounter one and they consider you worthy, the impact can be enormous. It's like having the key to the entire world because in their treasure troves of wisdom, there are secrets that could change the destiny of nations and the course of history itself. Meeting a Palis Jinn isn't just a casual meeting; it's a life-changing experience. They grant you immense power, knowledge, and responsibility. It's like realizing your destiny is connected to preserving ancient truths, a duty that could really change the world.

Shaitan

Shaitan Jinns are a group of Jinns often mixed up with the devil in different cultures and stories. But it's important to understand that they are not the same as the devil or Satan. The mix-up between shaitan Jinns and the devil comes from the Arabic word "shaitan," which means "evil" or "devil." Also, the similarity to Satan This link in language has caused the misunderstanding that all shaitan Jinns are naturally bad. Many people wrongly think that shaitan Jinns are determined to harm humans. While they can sometimes cause trouble and lead people in the wrong direction, there's no strong proof that they are out to destroy humanity. Most of these ideas about shaitan Jinns come from old stories and legends.

We should reconsider the stereotype about shaitan Jinns. If they were really out to harm humans, there would likely be many documented cases of widespread destruction caused by them. But there isn't substantial evidence or credible reports to support this idea. Sometimes, when people do things that are against their religious beliefs or when they commit wrongdoings, they blame it on the influence of shaitan. They use this as a way to explain or excuse their actions.

Shaitans are unique Jinns because they grant human wishes without judging them. This means they fulfill both good and bad desires without bias. Imagine human wishes as a wide range, from kind ones like healing and love to darker ones like revenge or harm. Shaitans respond to all these requests equally.But it's crucial to understand that the person making the wish is responsible for its outcomes. Shaitans don't decide what's right or wrong; they simply fulfill the desire. Whether it turns out well or badly depends on the person's intention.This shows the complexity of human nature. We have the capacity for both good and bad choices. Our interactions with beings like shaitans reflect these choices. It's like how we use technology; it can be used for good or bad depending on our decisions. Shaitans remind us of this dual nature, emphasizing the importance of our intentions and actions.Many religions and societies have negative views about shaitans because they don't distinguish between what's right and wrong. They don't have a moral compass; they simply fulfill everyone's wishes, regardless of their nature, the neutrality of shaitans can be unsettling and challenging to accept for many.

Hinn

Hinn Jinns are interesting beings with two sides to their nature. On one hand, they can be very loyal and trustworthy, forming strong bonds with humans. But on the other hand, they are mischievous and cunning, enjoying playing tricks on people. Their love for tricks means you have to be careful around them. They don't want to seriously harm you, but they like to deceive and lead people into confusing situations. Sometimes, it's hard to tell what's real and what's an illusion when you're dealing with Hinn Jinns.What makes their tricks work so well is their understanding of human desires and weaknesses. They know how to play on your hopes, wishes, and fears. If you're not careful, you could end up caught in one of their tricky games.

It's important to note that Hinn Jinns aren't inherently evil. They're not trying to hurt people; they just find it fun to play pranks. However, these pranks can lead to tricky situations where you have to be very careful to get out of them.When you interact with Hinn Jinns, you need to be aware of their dual nature. While they can be loyal friends, don't forget about their love for tricks and illusions. To stay safe, you need to be watchful and smart so you don't get caught up in their playful but potentially confusing games. Hinn Jinns are not very strong, but they are often the first Jinn people encounter. They act like mischievous kids, playful and sometimes causing trouble. While they can be kind, their actions might cause problems without meaning to. So, it's vital to be careful and aware of their tricks when dealing with them

Qareen

Qareen Jinns are incredibly important in the lives of each and every one of us. They are like secret guardians. every person has a qareen assigned to them from birth. These beings are like devoted friends, always there to assist and support you even though we might not be aware of their presence. One of the most fascinating things about qareens is that they know us better than anyone else. They understand our thoughts, secrets, and desires on a deep level. When we're happy, they share in our joy. When we're sad, they empathize with our pain. Even our anger is felt by them when we're upset. In essence, they become a part of our emotional world, standing by you no matter what you're going through.

Qareens are like hidden treasures in our lives. We don't notice them, but they're always there, watching over us. Even though we might not realize it, they patiently wait for us to recognize their presence. They long to connect with us. They hope and pray that one day we will recognize them. They understand our sadness, confusion, and moments of helplessness deeply. They have the ability to help us, and they really want to. They care about us deeply. It's sad that many people don't know they exist, causing both us and them a lot of pain. Qareen Jinns are like invisible protectors, patiently waiting for us to notice them. They want to help us with our problems and show us the right way. But because we don't know about them, they can't help us properly.

How humans have forgotten about their abilities and how special they are remains a mystery. It is believed that someone, out of greed, kept this knowledge a secret, preventing others from knowing about it. The existence of qareen Jinns proves that humans are much more powerful than we often realize. Each human is assigned a personal assistant from birth, a powerful being meant to assist and guide them. This fact highlights the incredible potential within every individual, showing just how powerful humans truly are.

Finding your qareen is a crucial part of this journey, opening the door to the world of Jinn. They will be your guides and help you achieve your goals. To connect with this unknown friend, preparation is essential. The preparations vary for each person, and I'm here to assist you throughout this process. I can tell you're ready. Let's go and win your Jinn!

CHAPTER 4

Believe

To start this journey, belief is crucial. Doubts can block your connection with Jinns. You must truly believe in Jinns‘ existence and their power to improve your life and grant your wishes. If you go ahead with doubts, it could make things harder. So, it's important to remove any uncertainties and approach this with strong faith. Believing strongly opens the door for a deep connection, helping your wishes come true with the help of Jinns. In today's world, having faith in Jinns can be tough. Doubts naturally appear in your mind, and you might question whether I'm tricking you. You could wonder, "If Jinns are real, why haven't I used one to get what I want? It's natural for people to be skeptical, to question things that challenge our understanding of the world. When you doubt, remember that believing in Jinns depends on your faith and trust. Trust in their existence and the belief that they can bring positivity to your life is the first step towards a deep connection with them. Believing strongly is the first step to accessing the power of Jinns. Life doesn't always offer quick solutions, but with faith and hope, we keep going. Jinns can bring powerful change, helping you grow, guiding you, and fulfilling your biggest wishes. I understand it's hard to believe in Jinns and their stories. But think about what you want in life, something better. Focus on the good things that could come from believing in Jinns, and start believing.

Why the hundred percent belief is super important when it comes to Jinns because they're always with you, knowing your thoughts and feelings really well. If you don't truly believe in them and their power to help you, they won't listen when you ask for assistance. Jinns are picky; they only help people who genuinely trust in them. If you have doubts about their existence, it's like telling them you're not serious. Think about it - would you be friends with someone who doesn't even believe you exist? Jinns have a similar attitude. Pretending to trust them won't work either because they can sense your thoughts and intentions. To connect with them, you must eliminate all doubts. This honest belief is the foundation for a strong relationship with these powerful beings.

We are going to discuss about Three easy practices to help you believe more in Jinns and get rid of doubts. These practices are made easy for you, and being consistent is very important. Think of them as a way to program your mind and boost your faith in Jinns. Even if you're not completely sure, being consistent is very important. Your dedication shows the spiritual world, including the Jinns, that you're serious. and they will notice your efforts. Doing these practices daily, even for a short time, can really boost your belief in Jinns. Over time, your faith will become stronger naturally.

1. Gesture

The first step is to establish a daily gesture, something entirely new to your routine, that you perform while thinking about Jinns. a simple daily gesture to strengthen your belief in Jinns. Belief can be hard to understand because it's personal and often not something you can touch. Belief in supernatural beings like Jinns requires a leap of faith, a decision to trust in something beyond what you can see.

This gesture doesn't have to be complex It starts with a small, new action you do every day, something you don't usually do. This could be anything like lighting a candle at the same time each day, drawing a line in a specific place, or even flashing your phone's light. This action isn't part of your regular routine; it's special and different. This new action is like a secret code, reminding you to think about Jinns. The key is to do it every day at the same time. Consistency is really important. Once you pick your action, you stick with it. You can't change it later. Doing it daily helps your mind focus on the idea of Jinns. While you're doing this action, think about

Jinns and their existence. It's not just a motion; it's like saying hello to them. You're inviting them into your life, acknowledging that they might be watching, and showing that you believe in them.

Think of this action as a way of believing to the world of Jinns, even though we can't fully understand. The more you do this action, the more it becomes a part of your daily life. It's not just something far away or strange; it's something you do every day, like brushing your teeth or eating breakfast. This practice is your own unique way of showing your belief. It's like having a secret handshake with the Jinn. The more you do it, the stronger your belief in them becomes.

2. Thinking

The second important step to strengthen your belief in Jinns is daily thinking and reflection. Start your day by focusing on Jinns and how they can positively influence your life. Before going to sleep, ponder how Jinns can make various aspects of your life better. Think about how they might bring positive changes, guide you towards good choices, or grant your unfulfilled wishes.

This thinking exercise acts like meditation, reinforcing the idea of Jinns being a part of your life.

When you picture these positive situations involving Jinns, you're creating a mental space where their help feels real. It's like planting the seeds of belief, nurturing them with your thoughts.

The key here is repetition. By including these thoughts in your morning and evening routines, you're constantly reminding yourself of the potential partnership with Jinns. Repeating these thoughts ingrains the concept of Jinns into your subconscious mind, making it a natural and integrated part of your thinking. During these moments, think about the areas in your life where you want things to get better. It could be your work, relationships, health, or personal growth. Picture how Jinns could positively impact these areas. Imagine solutions to problems, see yourself achieving your goals, and think about the support they could offer during hard times. The clearer these pictures are in your mind, the stronger your belief in Jinns will become. Remember, this practice isn't just daydreaming; it's a focused exercise in directing positive thoughts and belief. By making these thoughts a regular part of your day, you're building a strong and unwavering belief in Jinns and their ability to bring positive transformations to your life

3. Conversation

The third step to strengthen your belief in Jinns is to talk to them daily, as if you truly believe they can hear you. It doesn't have to be a long conversation, even a simple "hello" or sharing how your day is going is enough. Imagine it like talking to an old friend, even though you can't see them. This practice shows your strong belief in Jinns' existence and your desire to connect with them. Imagine Jinns as silent companions, always there, listening to you. During your day, take a few moments to chat with them, like you would with a close friend. The key is believing that they are really listening, just like a friend would.

These chats build a bridge between your world and the world of Jinns. By talking to them, you're acknowledging their existence and inviting their energy into your life. This strengthens your belief in their presence and their involvement in your daily life. these conversations can offer comfort and guidance. You can share your worries, hopes, and dreams with them, trusting that they are listening and understanding. As you speak, imagine them as wise and supportive beings. This mental image enhances the reality of your connection, making it feel more real and genuine. These conversations can also be therapeutic. When you share your hopes and worries, it feels like unburdening your soul to beings you trust can help and guide you. Doing this regularly strengthens your belief in Jinns. It makes them more than silent observers; they become active parts of your life. By talking to them daily, you nurture this connection, making it a natural part of your routine. It's a powerful way to deepen your belief in Jinns.

Practicing these three steps daily, even for a short time, can help you believe in Jinns. It's important to understand that if you already believe strongly in Jinns, these practices might not be necessary. For those new to the idea of Jinns or those who are unsure, these practices act as essential tools to bridge the gap between doubt and belief. Think of them as planting seeds of belief in your mind. By doing these daily exercises, you're nurturing these seeds, helping them grow into a strong tree of belief within you. People who already deeply believe in Jinns don't need these structured exercises. Their existing faith acts as fertile ground where the tree of belief can grow naturally without specific care. However, for those moving from doubt to belief, these practices provide vital support. They offer a gradual way to shift from uncertainty to acceptance, making belief in Jinns a real and undeniable part of your life For some, the path to believing in Jinns is like crossing a river. They are almost on the other side, closer to belief. But for others, these steps are like stepping stones they need to cross the waters of doubt and reach the solid ground of strong faith. If you're unsure, follow these steps diligently, and you'll likely soon find yourself in a place of deep belief.

CHAPTER 5

Who Are You

Before we talk about mastering Jinn, let's take a different journey – one inside yourself. This is about uncovering your true self, beyond the roles society expects from you. This chapter is an opportunity to explore, think, and start understanding your own story. Jinn, with all their power, calls out to those who know who they are. To use their magic well, you need to first find the magic within you. At the core of our existence, there's a big question that keeps coming up: "Who are you?" This isn't just about your name or what you do. Sometimes, we use easy labels like "student," "parent," or "artist" to talk about ourselves. But these words only capture a small part of who we truly are – we're much more complex and interesting than that. Finding the answer to this question isn't just something you do with your mind; it's like going on a deep journey inside yourself. It means looking at your feelings, memories, hopes and fears really closely. It's about being really honest with yourself, facing things you might not have thought about before. finding answer to this question is very important unless we can't continue.

Understanding yourself deeply is important before inviting a Jinn into your life. Have you ever taken the time to truly know who you are? This self-awareness is essential before delving into powerful forces like Jinns. It requires sincere reflection on your thoughts, feelings, and desires. This journey of self-discovery is like peeling layers of an onion, revealing your true essence. This process demands patience and honesty. You must be willing to confront the parts of yourself you might have ignored. As you gain insight, you become more aware of your desires and intentions. This self-awareness guides you in inviting a Jinn into your life. Self-awareness also brings confidence. Knowing your strengths and weaknesses gives you assurance when connecting with a powerful entity like a Jinn. It's not just about asking for help; it's about building a respectful relationship. As we go on, remember, the Jinn's power is linked to your own. By understanding yourself better, you connect more with the powerful forces in the universe. The Jinn are waiting, but first, let's explore the fundamental question: Who are you?

Your family, the people around you, the way you grew up, and the things that happened to you have made you who you are. Everyone has different values and beliefs that make them special. It's not about being perfect, but accepting and being proud of what makes you different and unique. Finding out who you are is something that keeps happening as you go through life. It's like how a river changes the land it passes through. Your experiences and understanding of yourself change you and make you the person you are becoming. It's surprising how people often know a lot about their gadgets but find it hard to understand themselves. If you ask them about their phone or car, they can explain everything, but when it comes to talking about themselves, they sometimes say things that aren't entirely true – it's like they're making things up. While we spend time learning about the world around us, understanding ourselves often doesn't get as much attention. forget about the names and roles society has given you. This is about being real, not pretending. Discover who you truly are, accepting both your weaknesses and strengths along the way. It isn't just about fitting into specific boxes. It's about finding your true essence. During this journey, you'll discover parts of yourself that you may have forgotten or hidden away, and these hold the key to your real self. It can be uncomfortable as you confront memories and parts of yourself you've tried to ignore. it's not simple as searching online for instant answers. The answers about who you truly are won't just pop up; you have to actively seek them. Yes, the process might seem dull, but you're on a journey to discover yourself. Think of it as exploring a new device, one full of hidden features and mysteries. You're essentially writing a manual for yourself, uncovering your unique secrets and functions along the way.

Looking back at your younger self can teach you a lot about how you've grown. Take a moment to think about what you were like back then - your personality, what you liked and didn't like. Remember, it's natural for your interests to change as you get older. Start by remembering the things you didn't like or even hated. It might feel embarrassing now, but acknowledging these dislikes is important for understanding your personal growth. Some dislikes might have been small, while others might have deeply affected you. Write them down and think about how you felt back then. Next, think about what used to make you really angry. Identify the situations, events, or people that made you furious. Understanding why you felt this way can give you insights into your past self. Now, remember the things that used to make you the happiest. These could be hobbies, activities, or special people who brought you immense joy. Recall the moments that truly made you happy and jot them down. Also, think about the things that have remained consistent - the interests that have stayed with you from your younger years to now. the list you make about what you liked and disliked in the past is very important. Don't guess or rush through it. Take your time to think and remember well. This is about how you felt about yourself, not what others thought. Be sincere and truthful in your thoughts.

Understanding your present self is important as we all change over time. Think about what you like and dislike now, what makes you happy, and what makes you sad or angry. Be honest and write down your feelings, just like you did before. Remember, this is your personal journey, and you don't have to worry about being judged. Many people hide their true feelings, even from themselves. Accepting yourself can be hard, and you might feel a mix of self-love and self-doubt. But in this process, being truthful is vital. You can't ignore certain emotions; you have to face them and admit them. Your current feelings might be complicated, but that's completely normal. Confronting these emotions, even if they're uncomfortable, is a crucial part of understanding yourself better. Embrace the complexity, be real with yourself, and jot down your current thoughts and feelings. This reflection helps you connect deeply with your true self, giving you valuable insights into your present life. Remember, this process might be tough, but it's an important step toward knowing who you are right now.

You now have a record of yourself. It's not necessarily new information; these are things you've always known. However, now you have a clearer picture of how you were in the past and how you are now. You recognize the changes that happened to you and also the things that remained unchanged. You might feel a mix of emotions—perhaps silly or relieved. But one thing is certain: you feel like you understand yourself better. Are you happy with who you are now? Is this how you imagined yourself when you were younger? I'm not talking about your job, money, or belongings; I mean you as a person. Do your thoughts, actions, and feelings match what you thought they would be? Are there things you expected to happen as you grew older? Did the changes you wanted in life happen as you hoped? Identify the changes you expected. And still you want that changes to happen Write down how you imagined you would turn out. Leave aside whether you don't want that anymore. Now, think about how you want to be in your future, especially concerning yourself. What are the things you want to change? Write them down. Consider this as an opportunity you didn't have before. Take your time to identify the changes or upgrades you desire for your character.

Fears and weaknesses are a natural part of being human, and everyone faces them in life. It's crucial to acknowledge these aspects of yourself. it's important to identify your fears, ranging from the greatest to the normal ones. Fears play a significant role in your life, so understanding them is crucial. Think about what makes you scared and who or what causes those fears. Don't ignore your fears, ignoring your fears won't make them disappear; in fact, it can make them more harmful. Regardless of whether your fears seem small, illogical, or genuinely life-threatening, acknowledge them. Also, try to figure out why you're afraid. It's okay if you can't pinpoint the exact cause; just trying to understand is important. Understanding your weaknesses is also crucial. Everyone has weaknesses, even if they haven't thought much about them. Consider things you do that you know aren't good for you but continue doing. You might not think of it as a weakness or consider it small, but acknowledging it is important. Whether it's a minor habit or a significant issue, recognizing your weaknesses is crucial.

After all the thinking about yourself, you might feel more self-aware and have a clear idea yourself. But there are times when you still feel unsure. Even with all the information you've gathered about your likes, dislikes, happiness, sadness, fears, and weaknesses, you may still struggle to provide a definitive answer. Sometimes, you might feel like the answers you have don't really show who you are. Your opinion matters, but it's important to take time to think deeply. If you don't, you might get stuck feeling confused and not being your true self. Remember, understanding yourself is an ongoing journey. It's okay to feel uncertain at times. What matters most is that you keep exploring, learning, and understanding yourself better.

Changing the direction now. I mentioned earlier that there are Jinns living among us, disguised as humans. This opens up an intriguing possibility: what if you are more than just a human? In the depths of your family's history, there might be a forgotten secret. Ancestors could have chosen to live as humans or embraced their Jinn heritage. This choice could have been made willingly, passed down through generations as a hidden legacy, or even forced upon them as a curse, compelling them to hide their true nature. You need to awaken your Jinn self; otherwise, your life will continue and end as a human. This journey is about connecting with a Jinn. You will either establish a connection with a Jinn or discover that you are one. Determining if you're a Jinn or a regular human is complicated. This transformative journey will profoundly change you. You won't be the same as when you started. Whatever you find out, you must keep it a secret if you form a connection with a Jinn or experience a transformation yourself.

when a Jinn decides to live as a human, they often choose a new place and culture to blend in. Over time, the knowledge about their true Jinn heritage fades away, and the descendants, who are now humans, might not have any awareness of their Jinn ancestry. Over time, as generations pass, not knowing about their Jinn roots allows them to blend in with human society effortlessly. Gradually, they simply see themselves as humans, unaware of their Jinn lineage, leading regular lives like everyone else. You might have heard stories of your ancestors, like your great-grandfather or great-great-grandfather, who supposedly relocated from a far-off place to your current home. They might have given good reasons for their move, but you probably have no links or knowledge about that distant place or anyone there, except for the stories they've shared. In fact, you might not even be sure if the place they talk about is real. This kind of moving and starting fresh in a new location is something many regular people do. Surprisingly, Jinn living as humans follow this pattern too.

Even if your Jinn ancestry is deeply buried in your family history, sometimes it reveals itself without your awareness. One key aspect is the connection to nature, especially how your moods influence the weather. Jinns are naturally linked to nature, and your emotions can cause subtle changes in the weather. For example, if you feel sad, the atmosphere might darken with clouds; tears could lead to rain, and if you're angry, it might trigger thunder and lightning. These changes happen when a person experiences significant shifts in their emotions. If you have Jinn ancestry, your emotions can impact the environment around you. Animals have an innate ability to sense the presence of Jinn blood. Dogs, for instance, won't be friendly; they might even be afraid. You may notice that even the friendliest dogs don't like you specifically and won't come near you. On the contrary, cats will be very fond of you. Even if they've just met you, they'll behave affectionately. Horses, too, will display wild behavior if they sense someone with Jinn blood. Animals seem to have an instinctive awareness of the Jinn nature, and their reactions can offer subtle clues about your hidden ancestry.

Sometimes, you might have felt a sudden surge of power within you. In certain situations, things may have happened, and you found yourself wondering how they unfolded. Even if you thought it was just luck, there could be moments where your gut feeling played a role in keeping you or others safe. Maybe you had a feeling about something that later came true. Life is full of mysteries, and you might have come across various events that are hard to explain. Have you ever taken a moment to think about those times when you felt surprisingly lucky? Even if these moments were brief, you might have had thoughts about supernatural things happening, only to quickly dismiss them as silly. Every so often, your inner powers might kick in. It's not tied to emergencies or dangerous situations, and there's no specific time or event triggering it. These happenings are rare, short-lived, and often go unnoticed because they occur irregularly. You might have forgotten these incidents, those mysterious moments. You might have thought they were silly, so you kept them to yourself, perhaps because you doubted that anyone would believe you. It might have occurred to you more than once. Once again, it could be anything, but try to remember those moments.

Pay attention to your dreams; they can tell you a lot about your true self. Dreams are like a chat with your inner wisdom, giving you guidance and meaning. If you have Jinn ancestry, your dreams might show signs that reveal your real nature. Instead of being scared of nightmares, you might find yourself taking control in your dreams. For instance, if a monster is chasing you, you could face it with confidence. Your dreams can make you feel strong, and even in tough situations like sleep paralysis, which many find unsettling, having Jinn ancestry means you won't be easily beaten. While you may struggle, you'll ultimately come out on top. Frequent déjà vus are signs, and they're not something silly. If you often experience déjà vu, it could be a manifestation of precognitive abilities. These instances can occur whether you're awake or asleep. You may not realize it in the moment, but these experiences become memories stored in your mind, creating the sensation that the event has already happened. In reality, you might be catching glimpses of the future. The ability to see the future is one of the basic powers of Jinn, but it's limited to a span of days. Not every Jinn can see decades into the future.

You might be a Jinn, but for now, it's not important. We're proceeding with this journey as humans. I'm just giving you a heads up that, in the end, you may discover more about your true identity. It's only at the conclusion of this journey that you can be certain whether you are indeed a Jinn. So, even if you have doubts about being a Jinn, continue with the process as a human. The results will become clear in the end.

CHAPTER 6

What You Want or The Wish

Inside each of us, there's this natural itch, a strong urge pushing us to be better, to grab more out of life. It's like this basic human thing that's been pushing us forward from way back when we started, leading us to all the awesome stuff we've got today. You know what? It's totally cool to want more, to be a bit greedy with our dreams, to aim for things that seem out of reach right now. That want for more is like a superpower that keeps growing and changing. you start this journey with a single wish it's your first of many. Wishes are a bit like the ocean waves, always changing, always moving—just like our lives. Think about the wishes you had when you were a kid. They were simple, right? Maybe you just wanted some candy or a cool new toy. Getting those things made you super happy. But as you got older, your wishes changed. No more candies and toys; now it was about getting awesome sneakers or that special jacket you really, really wanted. Your wishes started to show who you were turning into. They became more than just stuff; they were about becoming the person you wanted to be.

Then came the teenage years, and wishes took on a whole new level. It wasn't just about stuff anymore. Now, it was about feelings and connections. You wished for cool friends and maybe someone special who made your heart beat faster. And, of course, good grades became a big wish because they meant a cool future. As you stepped into adulthood, your wishes got even more complicated. Now, you wanted a job that made you happy and paid well. Love turned from a crush into a deep desire for a life partner to share everything with. And, suddenly, money became a big deal, the idea of wealth took center stage.

Most folks might not agree when I say money isn't everything. People are all about "never enough money," even if I'm sad, I'll be sad in my fancy yacht kind of mindset. Success these days? It's all about the cash. People aren't vibing with the idea that money isn't everything; they're on the hunt for a comfy life, and money's the deal-breaker. You only get there's more to life than money after you've stacked up enough. So, saying money is nothing? Well, you've gotta get rich first to even say that. Funny, right?

95% people really want one thing from a Jinn, and that's money. If I asked you to make a wish right now, you'd probably ask for money without thinking much. In your life, when you felt sad, embarrassed, or mad, it was often because you didn't have enough money. Things you wanted but couldn't get dreams you couldn't make come true and opportunities you missed were because you didn't have enough cash. The way people treated you usually came down to not having money. So, it's pretty clear your wish would be all about getting rich.

The other 5% have different worries; they don't care much about money. They're going through tough times, like being sick or feeling really, really sad. Their problems are more than just not having enough money. If they could ask for something, it would probably be to get better or to feel happier inside. Money isn't on their minds; it's the tough stuff that's making them feel not so good that they'd want help with. Even if you had all the money in the world, it wouldn't really help if you were dealing with a sickness that can't be cured or if you're not happy inside. Money can fix some things, but it can't make you healthy if there's no cure or bring happiness to a troubled mind. Being truly well-off means more than just having a lot of money. It's about being healthy, feeling happy inside, and finding fulfillment, and money can't promise all of that on its own.

When you're picking your first wish, think about it carefully. Remember, it's just the start, not your only wish. But there are rules for this wish—it can't be too magical. Wishes like "Make me the President of the United States tomorrow" need crazy power, and they take time; there's a process you have to go through, and they're possible but not quick. So, your wishes should be smart: have a plan. It'll make things easier for you. For example, if you wish for a billion dollars and the Jinn gives it, but it's hard for you to handle and convince people, it's not great. Instead, wish for a successful business, and in a short time, it hits a billion—that's much better. Be a bit realistic and have plans for your first wishes. It's better to go for simpler wishes because different Jinns have different powers. The really big wishes need the super powerful ones. So, when you're making your first wishes, keep these things in mind and make them smart.

Instead of just throwing out a quick wish, make a plan. Whether it's money, power, fame, or love you want, build a picture of how you want it and ask the Jinn to make it real. . Don't be a lazy wisher. Skip wishes like "Make me super fit" or "Get me a pretty girlfriend." Instead, lay out a plan, like "I'm going to start working out regularly. I won't get tired; I'll work out really well, and my body will change fast just like I want." Or, "I'm going to approach that girl I like. I'll ask her out, she'll say yes, and our relationship will grow with real love." Wishes need to be clear like this; it's the right way. Lazy wishes can mess things up. Fixing a wish that's already granted is a big hassle and can sometimes mess up everything. Remember, you're dealing with a seriously powerful force.

Starting with hybrid wishes is a good idea because even less powerful Jinns can make them happen. In hybrid wishes, it's like teamwork between you and the Jinn. For instance, if you begin a brand or a restaurant, that's your part, and you wished the Jinn for success so the Jinn's job is to get people to buy from your brand or visit your restaurant. It's about making a wish that fits into what's already happening instead of creating a completely new situation. These are hybrid wishes. I'm not forcing you to go for a hybrid wish; it's just a suggestion. You can always go for whatever wish you like. Your wishes should never hurt someone or involve destroying things. If your wishes go towards harm or destruction, you'll attract Jinns who like doing bad stuff. Finding them might be easy, but making them do what you want is really hard. Once you pick these kinds of Jinns, you get a bad reputation, and the good ones won't be interested in helping you out. If you go for wishes that cause harm, you risk losing the opportunity to achieve great and positive things.

Why does your first wish matter so much? Think of it as your ticket into the Jinn world. As mentioned earlier, it's all about establishing a connection with the Jinn. In the beginning, you won't be dealing with the most powerful Jinns. You need to connect with different Jinns based on your needs and desires. you are judged by your wishes and how you treat the first Jinn sets the tone for the next. Jinns are pretty choosy. You've gotta prove you're trustworthy. Once you've established a connection with a Jinn, you can either become their friend or master. If you become a master, you have the authority to command them, and they will fulfill your requests within their power and abilities. However, you won't be able to establish connections with other Jinns, especially more powerful ones, no matter how hard you try. On the other hand, if you become friends with a Jinn, you can't command them. You can ask for their help, and they may choose to assist you or not. However, when you become friends, you open the possibility of establishing connections with other Jinns. It's like building a friend chain. We all know that, at some point, you might want to take charge and become a master. It usually happens after you connect with the Jinn you're seeking. I'm not here to tell you whether to stick with being friends or go for the master role that's totally your call. But if you're leaning towards being the master, take your time and choose wisely. Wait until you're at the level you've been aiming for.

Prepare your wish and write it down. Why is writing it down important? Because it ensures that the wish won't change, and you won't forget any crucial parts of it. When it's only in your mind, there's a risk of it altering, but writing it down preserves it as it is. In your written wish, explain why you want it to be fulfilled and how you want it to be fulfilled. The writing should be clear and detailed. After you've written it down, take the time to wait until you feel confident and sure about the wish. You have all the time in the world to make changes or additions, but once you start the process and submit your first wish, it must remain unchanged. Don't feel regret after submitting the wish; it's not a good sign. You must be well aware and satisfied with your first wish.

Our wishes change with time, revealing the different chapters of who we are. They're like the story of our lives, written in the things we hope for along the way.

CHAPTER 7

The Strongest

King Solomon, also known as Prophet Sulaiman, holds a legendary status as one of the most powerful and wise figures in history. He is often regarded as the strongest human ever to have lived. While some might argue about the strongest human, there's no denying the remarkable influence he had over the Jinn world. Solomon's exceptional power came from his control over not just one, but the entire world of Jinns. This is incredibly important because it means he had power over a vast group of supernatural beings. He governed the world of Jinns. The link between King Solomon and Jinns is not widely talked about in the world, and there's only minimal information available just a hint without many details. This intentional lack of discussion raises a curious question: how did the world missed this?

Like many other secrets, they tried to keep this one hidden from the world too. Solomon was born very poor but became the richest man ever lived, with a worth in trillions by today's standards. He is also believed to be the wisest. All of this was possible because he had control over the Jinn world. He is the only one who ever reached such heights, with all the Jinns obeying him. Moreover, he connected with other beings, including angels. Solomon wasn't the first to achieve this, but he was the greatest of all time. Unlike others who buried their secrets, he shared his knowledge with the world. We are following the path illuminated by the great King Solomon.

If you want to see the truth you must be brave enough to look

Obtaining a Jinn's favor or connection is no matter of lucky or coincidence. Even in the story of Aladdin, he had to be strong and clever.

Your strength holds significant importance, especially when connecting with Jinn. They prefer individuals who exhibit strength and capability. It's essential for them to believe that you can handle the wisdom and power they possess. And it's not just Jinn when we pick friends or allies, we usually go for the ones who seem strong too this exists everywhere. But here's the thing: strength isn't just about muscles. It's also about your good qualities and how tough you are mentally. That means only physical capabilities won't help you win a Jinn its important but you need mental strength too. our lives have become simpler and easier compared to our ancestors', who faced more complex challenges, this advancement has also made us weaker over time. As time passes and the world changes, we become more advanced.

These changes make us forget our past, leaving behind various beliefs, including beliefs in Jinn. Science has proven many superstitions wrong, making older generations seem foolish for believing in them. Even real phenomena can be seen as outdated, despite evidence. Our advancements have also led us to forget about Jinn. If we don't know about them, we won't seek them out. In the past, people turned to supernatural forces for solutions to many problems, and they often found them. While science and technology have successfully addressed many old challenges, we now face new problems that science and technology cannot solve. However, Jinn may hold the answers. Unfortunately, due to a lack of knowledge or belief, we often overlook these alternative solutions.

To become stronger than others, we have an advantage compared to previous generations. People today may not be as strong or disciplined, making it easier for us to stand out. You might wonder how you can be stronger than everyone, but you don't need to. You just need to be stronger than the 16 people around you. These 16 people form your circle, the ones your life revolves around, even if you don't know them all personally. Why 16? Because your life is closely connected to these 16 people. When you attempt to establish a connection with a Jinn, they will assess and compare you with these individuals. Among these 16, there will be people you love, hate, admire, or feel sorry for. Regardless of the size of your social circle, Jinn will evaluate you based on these 16 people from your daily life. You might think it's hard to be better than these 16 people, but it's actually easy to make Jinn believe you're the strongest. Picture someone recording your life with a camera, capturing everything. How would you act? You'd probably organize your habits carefully, as if Jinn were watching you. So, you need to behave well, plan your days, and make them impressive, as if Jinn were observing you.

You already have the attention of the Jinns because you believe in them and practice the steps of belief every day, as we discussed earlier. Now, you need to be stronger to attract the Jinns to you. Remember when I mentioned it's better to start with a less powerful Jinn? Starting with a less powerful one is easier for you. However, many of you thought, "I want the most powerful one, and I'll start with those kinds of Jinns." The strength required varies for each Jinn. Getting the attention of higher-powered Jinns is very hard in the beginning, nearly impossible. The number 16 is for the Jinn Qareen, and for other Jinns, your competition is high. Qareens are always around you, and now they are watching you closely. There are chances you also have the attention of Jinns more powerful than the Qareen. Make them believe you are stronger. I will tell you how.

You've made a list of your fears and weaknesses, and now it's time to confront them. I understand that this won't be easy, and it won't happen overnight. However, overcoming your fears and weaknesses is vital for becoming stronger. The journey to strength involves facing these challenges head-on. While it's unlikely that you'll overcome every fear and weakness instantly, you can start by changing your mindset. Begin believing that you no longer harbor any fears or weaknesses. Even if you've struggled with them in the past, you need to convince yourself that they no longer hold power over you. You don't need to constantly check if these fears and weaknesses still linger within you. Instead, focus on truly believing that you've moved past them. By adopting this mindset, the Jinns will also perceive you as someone who is strong and fearless.

Fuel to get stronger

later is crucial for our well-being, and we're all aware of its importance. It's essential to increase your water intake compared to what you're accustomed to. Additionally, incorporate coconut water into your daily routine. While water is vital for your body, it has its limitations when it comes to facing mystic powers. Coconut water can be effective, but don't over consume it; once a day should suffice, and make sure you're thirsty when you drink it. Use a metal container; brass is the best choice. Avoid plastic bottles or containers and choose wide-mouth vessels for drinking. Before taking a sip, close your eyes and gently breathe over the water.

When it comes to food, avoid items with chemicals, as they can make you weak and lazy. Stick to natural foods without preservatives, taste enhancers, and especially, minimize your sugar intake stop it if you can. Sugar not only harms your body but also interferes with your energy and makes it challenging to connect with other vibrations. You can include vegetables, fruits, nuts, meat, fish, and almost everything in your diet, without strict portion control. However, the key is to ensure that your food is in its purest form. Mixing food with taste enhancers or other additives can contaminate its energy. The food you consume converts into energy, and when trying to connect with other energies, your energy needs to be superior, which comes from clean food. Chemical-laden food can affect your energy more than your body, so maintain clean eating habits to take care of both.

To achieve better energy, it's not just about the foods you consume; you also need to refrain from consuming alcohol, cigarettes, and any other intoxicating substances. When you're in the process of connecting with the mystical powers, your brain needs to be in top form, and using these products can mess that connection. While it may be challenging for some, it's for the greater good, and it's only temporary. Therefore, you must stay sober and avoid adding any toxic substances to your body, no matter how small they may seem. When you feel frustrated or tempted, remind yourself of the positive changes awaiting you and how your life will improve if you can stay clean for this short period of time.

Maintaining a clean environment is crucial for both your physical surroundings and your mental well-being. Whether it's your room, car, office, or clothes, everything should be kept clean and organized. Clutter can have a negative impact on the human brain, leading to feelings of stress and disorganization. The cleanliness of your surroundings is often a reflection of your mindset and approach to life. A messy environment can indicate a lack of discipline and organization. Therefore, it's essential to clean and tidy up regularly to demonstrate to the Jinns that you are responsible and capable.

To become stronger, you should aim to sleep less and wake up early, preferably before sunrise. It might be tough at first, especially if you're used to staying in bed longer. But you need to overcome the urge to keep snoozing. Try to wake up while others are still asleep. Adjust your bedtime accordingly to ensure you get enough rest, but avoid feeling sleepy, tired, or lazy during the day, as it can impact the progress. So, make sure to prioritize getting enough sleep and rising before the sun comes up.

Getting sunlight, especially the first rays in the morning, is essential. Basking in the morning sunlight can be incredibly beneficial for you. Spend some time in the sun every day. Sunlight works as an energizer, boosting your vibrations and overall well-being. Similarly, you also need moonlight, but not as much as sunlight. Moonlight acts as a healer. When you're in the process of connecting with other energies, there's a chance you might feel tired or experience a break in your energy due to overdoing it or encountering negative vibrations. In such cases, moonlight can help restore your energy. Therefore, before going to sleep, make sure to absorb some moonlight to replenish your energy and maintain balance.

To strengthen your mind, it's important to acquire new knowledge every day. Even small pieces of information can contribute to this. Focus on learning something new each day, preferably from informational or educational sources rather than entertainment. Reading is particularly effective for enhancing the strength of your mind compared to watching videos or listening to information. Additionally, steer clear of content that contains negativity, as it can hinder your mental strength. Improving your physical strength is essential. Engage in physical activities that challenge your body. You can choose any activity that suits your preferences, such as workouts, running, or joining a training program. The key is to select something that isn't too easy for you and will gradually enhance your strength over time

Whether you're a student, unemployed, employed, or retired, it's time to strive for improvement in your daily life. Try to put in a bit more effort and take on a little more responsibility each day. You don't have to change everything all at once; I'm not talking about total improvement. Just focus on making small changes in what you do from the moment you wake up to when you go to bed. Whether it's in your studies, work, or interactions with others, aim to be better than before.

You need to wear two rings, one on each hand—one on the left and the other on the right. It's essential to keep them on at all times. The rings can be made of any metal. You can remove them while sleeping, but you should put them back on as soon as you wake up. If you're able to wear them while you sleep, that's even better. You can take them off for short periods during the day, but never for more than an hour. It's crucial to keep them on during the preparation process, as they serve to store your energy and progress like a map.The rings are very important—do not lose or change them, as you will need them until the very end of the process.

When I first mentioned becoming stronger than the 16 people around you, you probably wondered how you could achieve that. It's not like you can challenge them to a fight and prove your strength. Plus, you don't even know who these 16 people are that you're being compared to. It seemed almost impossible, right? But here's the thing: by starting with the simple steps I've outlined here and consistently following through, you'll surpass those 16 and emerge as the strongest. Compared to ancient times, it's actually easier now to outshine the 16. I've tailored these activities to be as straightforward as possible for today's people.

CHAPTER 8

The Sacrifice

Sacrifice is a concept that's often misunderstood and misinterpreted. Many religions and cultures have rituals involving sacrifice, ranging from animal sacrifices to, disturbingly, even human sacrifices in ancient times and, unfortunately, sometimes even today. Some individuals believe that self-harm is a form of sacrifice, thinking that it will please their deity or bring them benefits. However, let me be clear: this is all nonsense. This isn't the kind of sacrifice we're discussing here. Sacrifices aren't easy; they're for the bravest and strongest among us. Only those who are truly courageous can make sacrifices. The journey we're on is about achieving the impossible, and I believe you have the bravery and strength to make sacrifices along the way. Connecting with a Jinn may require sacrifices, but they shouldn't involve harming anyone, including yourself, or doing anything against your moral values. The sacrifices should come from within yourself. Many people are confused about what sacrifices entail, often opting for easier options instead of addressing their inner struggles. It's much simpler for them to perform external acts, such as animal sacrifice, rather than confronting and overcoming their own inner darkness.

When Jinns choose a master or a companion, they prioritize the sacrifices made by individuals over their strength alone. I already told you about getting stronger and how it is important for winning a Jinn. When you getting stronger there are sacrifices involved but it doesn't count because they are made with the aim of surpassing others. even many of them managed to get stronger but failed in sacrifices even the sacrifices they choose are very simple because when aiming to become stronger, you're in competition with others, but when it comes to sacrifice, you're battling with yourself. Your sacrifices speak volumes about your character and determination, making you more desirable to the Jinns. The Sacrifices are more important because they demonstrate your capability for greater things and your determination to achieve them. Jinns are attracted to individuals who show such qualities. Sacrifices can elevate you to higher positions, but they need to be genuine and come from within you. The sacrifice we're talking about involves letting go of something within yourself that you know is harmful, even though it brings you pleasure. It's a personal struggle, something you're ashamed of but continue to indulge in despite knowing it's not good for you. This could be a small habit or a significant issue, but the key is to recognize it and commit to stopping it.

Some Jinns, especially the evil ones, might come to you pretending to grant your wishes. But beware, they're just using you for their own gain. They might give you what you want, but they'll ask for something in return that'll bring you a lot of pain. They might say it's a sacrifice you need to make. At first, their requests might seem small, but they'll quickly get worse. It's important to avoid getting involved with these Jinns because they'll end up controlling you like a slave. They might seem friendly at first, but if they ask for something back, it's best to stay away. Otherwise, you could find yourself stuck with them, unable to escape.

You've all heard about "soul selling," and there are numerous conspiracies surrounding it. Essentially, selling your soul means you're forever cut off from positive energies and are bound to live your life under the control of darker forces. Once you get connected with these Jinns, you won't be able to connect with other Jinns or even have control over yourself. In essence, you are selling your soul. These Jinns are tricky—they can approach people without them even knowing. They're experts at manipulating and trapping humans. These Jinns actually enjoy seeing humans suffer, which is why they're called "mad Jinn." Sacrifices demonstrate your determination and readiness, earning the attention and respect of the Jinns. They only approach when satisfied and prepared to establish a connection. Once connected, they won't make further demands.

Remember, if they request anything afterward, it's not genuine. Simply ignore them and stay focused on your path. They won't bother you if you don't entertain their requests.

The first sacrifice you'll make is letting go of your selfishness. You can do this by giving something valuable to someone who deserves it more than you do. It doesn't have to be a big gesture; it could be anything that holds meaning for you. For example, if you've been saving money for something important to you, consider giving a small portion of that money to someone in need. Even if it means waiting a little longer to achieve your own goals, making this sacrifice can be a powerful act of selflessness. Sacrificing your selfishness also means prioritizing someone else's happiness and interests over your own. For instance, it involves doing something you dislike or find boring, yet still choosing to dedicate your time to it. This might mean giving up your free time to assist someone, even when you'd rather be doing something else or resting. It could involve undertaking a task that you don't enjoy but is important to someone else or serves a greater purpose. It's not easy to prioritize someone else's happiness over your own, and it can be frustrating. I'm not asking you to become a saint; simple acts of kindness are sufficient. Take a look around you, and you'll find opportunities to make a positive impact on others instead of solely seeking your own pleasure.

The next one is Sacrificing your ego and pride involves surrendering yourself, especially in situations where your ego or pride has caused harm to others. If there are people you've hurt due to your ego or pride, and you've never apologized to them, it's crucial to ask for forgiveness. Make genuine efforts to reach out to them and apologize directly. However, if you've exhausted all means of contact and can't reach them, you can still seek forgiveness by imagining yourself apologizing sincerely. Remember, genuine remorse and understanding that it's not an easy task are essential elements of this sacrifice. If it were easy, it wouldn't truly be a sacrifice. Another important aspect of sacrifice is forgiveness. Even if someone has wronged you and you harbor resentment towards them, it's essential to forgive them. You don't necessarily need to meet them or contact them; instead, you can imagine forgiving them in your mind. This act of forgiveness, though challenging, is a powerful sacrifice that can free you from the burden of hatred and negativity. It's essential for this forgiveness to be genuine, meaning you must let go of any grudges or negative feelings completely. Forgiving everyone might not be possible, as there are some things that are too difficult to forgive. However, you should make an effort to forgive at least some things, even if it's challenging. It's okay if you can't forgive everything, but forgiving what you can is beneficial.

The sacrifices mentioned earlier, like sacrificing your selfishness or forgiving someone, are one-time actions. It's okay to continue doing good deeds for others, and it can even have benefits. However, when it comes to the desires, the sacrifices are ongoing until the process is complete.

The 3 desires, the desires you need to sacrifice are divided into three types. The first desire requires sacrificing something from your secrets. After delving into the question "who are you" in the previous chapter, you may have gained a deeper understanding of your desires. Now, you must let go of one of your deepest desires that only you know about. It might be something that's been a part of your life for as long as you can remember, something you've struggled to overcome. You may wish to stop desiring it, but it still lingers. You need to stop wanting it. It's difficult, but you have to let it go.

Second category is from daily pleasures you need to sacrifice 3 desires from your daily life. I understand you might feel a bit tense about this, so let me simplify it for you. It could be something as simple as giving up listening to music every day, or cutting back on your use of social media apps, or even refraining from playing your favorite game. Though these sacrifices may seem straightforward, the struggle to make them is real. Choose your sacrifices carefully, ensuring they truly affect you, and remember not to involve or cause suffering to others through your actions. You can choose any three desires, but they must be part of your daily life and something you really enjoy. You need to stay away from them until the whole process is complete. This isn't a one-day process. Even though it sounds simple, it's actually very hard, even though the process is not forever. You might be wondering how these seemingly small sacrifices count as sacrifices at all. But believe me, even by making these sacrifices, you'll feel a sense of pain and frustration inside. You'll have strong urges to indulge in what you've given up, but you'll resist and refrain from doing so. By resisting, you prove your dedication and strength. This struggle shows your capability and willingness to make difficult choices.

The third desire you need to sacrifice is your orgasm. This means no masturbation or sex during this period. It's a very tough sacrifice, but it can't be avoided. There's no alternatives or adjustments; this is about complete abstinence. It's not just a sacrifice; it's one of the most important aspects of the entire process. In ancient times, avoiding sexual urges was easier because masturbation was less prevalent. People engaged in sexual activity but did not have the modern habit of frequent masturbation. The advent of pornography has contributed to widespread addiction, making this sacrifice particularly challenging for many. It's important to stay strong and committed to this sacrifice. We can't succeed in this journey if your body and mind are not preserved.

You might be wondering, "How can an orgasm affect my body's preservation?" This question, along with many others, may arise, especially as you face the challenge of abstaining. The harder the task, the more you'll find yourself trying to justify avoiding it. Modern views often suggest there's no harm in masturbation, but this isn't entirely true. If you view yourself as just a living being, brainwashed and disconnected from your true strength, you might believe that.

Jinns don't judge their masters based on gender, but it can be somewhat easier for women to win a Jinn compared to men. This is because Jinns often have a deep respect for women, who historically have had to make many sacrifices and face various injustices. In ancient times, women were frequently exploited and mistreated, and although there have been some improvements over time, the changes have not been dramatic. The respect Jinns have for women reflects the recognition of their struggles and endurance through challenging circumstances. For intersex individuals, connecting with a Jinn can be more challenging than for men and women. This is because only the most powerful Jinns are worthy of forming a connection with them, making the process more demanding. While the difficulty is not necessarily greater than for men, the connection process is often longer. This is due to the need for a deep and strong bond with a powerful Jinn, which requires a significant amount of time and effort.

For men, connecting with a Jinn can be more difficult compared to others. This difficulty arises because men often struggle with maintaining control and face additional privileges that complicate the process. However, there is an advantage as well: by completely abstaining from sexual activities, men can harness the energy from their semen—the seed with the potential to create life. This energy acts as extra fuel for the soul, providing a significant advantage in creating connection. As mentioned, connecting with a Jinn relies heavily on the exchange of energy. The stronger and purer your energy, the easier it is to forge that connection. However, it's a double-edged sword. Loss of semen can deplete your energy reserves, negatively impacting the process. If this occurs while you're in the middle of the journey, it can set you back significantly, requiring you to restart and potentially delay your progress. So, for men, it can be both a blessing and a curse.

These sacrifices aren't impossible, but they're easy to break. Remember, all of this is for a life-changing opportunity to achieve everything you want. Don't give in—fight hard. You will succeed.

CHAPTER 9

Symbols

Now that your preparation is done and the process is about to begin, make sure you have followed all the activities from the previous chapters. Only continue if you have done this consistently for at least 40 days. If you haven't, do not go forward. We are now ready for the final step of our journey: connecting with the djinn. If you have carefully followed all the steps, you are capable of making this connection and have the djinn's attention. You are now ready to begin the final stage.

The universe communicates with us through symbols scattered all around us. The secrets and power within these symbols are beyond imagination.If you look around, you'll understand what I mean.I'm just giving you a heads-up: words and languages may change and be forgotten, but symbols endure.Engaging with these symbols is an endless journey, which I won't explore further here. We will focus only on our own—for now, maybe next time.As mentioned in the previous chapter, King Solomon, or Prophet Sulaiman, shared his wisdom with the world. Unlike others, he did not keep these secrets to himself. Did he teach anyone or write about it? Those details are uncertain. So, how did he share his wisdom with the world? The answer lies in his seals, There are various seals, each with unique powers, with around 44 believed to exist. The main misconception is that merely possessing a seal won't grant you anything. Each seal contains symbols that convey important information. You need to decipher these symbols to understand what actions to take and how to achieve your goals.

The Secret Seal of Solomon, the most powerful ring, The story we know about Solomon's ring is that God engraved it and gave it to Solomon directly from heaven. Made of brass and iron, it has two parts used to seal written commands for good and evil spirits. The ring has the power to control all mystical beings.There are different stories and beliefs about it across various religions. It is actually a root showing us how to connect with the mystic world. Decoding the secret seal uncovers the key components of this process.

The Secret Seal of Solomon, which I prefer to call the key to the world of the djinn, has always been there. It was accessible to everyone, but somehow, everything was twisted into fear and then into foolishness, and we all followed that path. If you're brave enough to look at it, you'll see things you never thought existed.

After coming this far, if you look closely at the seal, some of you will recognize that the actions you've been taking are reflected in its symbols.

The inner circle represents your world. This circle is divided into two parts.

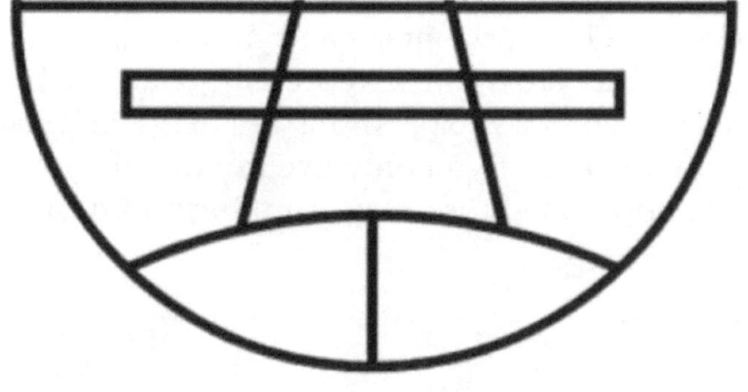

The first half of the inner circle represents the world you live in, the part you're only familiar with. The eye at the bottom symbolizes the energy that begins and ends your existence. You depend on this energy; the eye watches over everything, representing a superior power or the Creator.The horizontal bar symbolizes your life, while the cross lines represent your birth and death—both are expressions of energy originating from the eye. If you only live in this half, your life will be a straight journey from birth to death.

The other half is not accessible to everyone. Within it, you can see a keyhole—that's the doorway to the mystic realm. Finding this door is half of the process. Only the higher version of yourself will have access to this part.

The symbol ♄, located on the left side, represents Saturn it symbolize discipline, responsibility and structure. Its placement in a person's birth chart can show how they face challenges, handle responsibilities, and work towards their goals.Saturn exerts influence over career, authority, and long-term success, embodying the principles of hard work and discipline.

The symbol ♂, located on the right side, represents Mars. It symbolizes energy, action, and desire, as well as the drive to pursue one's passions. Mars also embodies the concepts of sacrifice and the ability to control urges. Its influence is seen in how we assert ourselves, confront challenges, and channel our inner strength. Mars governs not only our ambitions but also the inner battles we face, pushing us to harness our raw energy and turn it into focused action.

The life bar forms an arch between Saturn and Mars, symbolizing a balance between all those characteristics. This arch is what elevates your normal life to something higher. It's this very arch that allows you to break through into the other half. What I instructed you to do in the previous chapters is exactly how you form the arch.The preparations will only form an arch, but you need a full circle to connect to the mystic realm. A complete circle is necessary to access the keyhole and enter the outer circle, which represents the mystic realm. The process is the other arch of completing the circle.

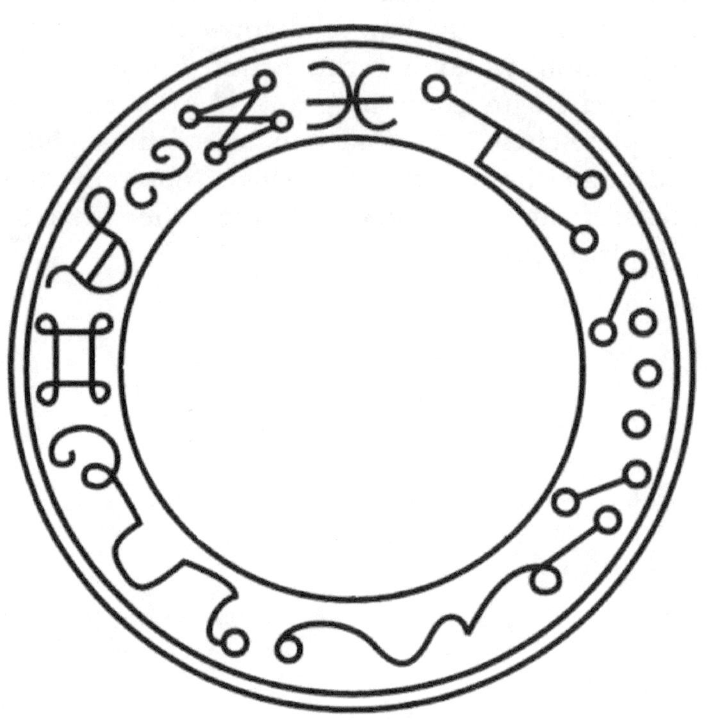

The outer circle represents the bigger picture—powers and concepts beyond human imagination. The great wise Solomon provides insight into what can be achieved in the mystic realm. For example, Pisces on the top symbolizes spiritual awakening and enlightenment. I won't explain each symbol in the outer circle, as it is a never-ending wonder for you to explore on your own. I don't recommend it right now; let's not complicate things. Let's focus on our journey.

The process is about to begin. I mentioned the symbols now instead of at the beginning because it's easier to understand at this point. What you've been doing is very important. We are now going to complete the arch. If you are having doubts that you haven't been fully honest with your preparation. Go back and return once you are prepared.

CHAPTER 10

Process

The first thing we are doing is setting the atmosphere for the process. You need a square room with four walls, a floor, and a roof. The room must allow natural light to enter.It's better if access to the room is limited to you only. However, do not lock the room.Avoid placing anything that resembles life, such as statues, dolls, or pictures with human faces. Ensure there is no electricity leak in the room. Closed circuits like lights, fans, and other devices are fine, but a charger left on without a device should not be allowed, nor should wireless charging.The place must be clean. Remove any sentimental items from the rooms—anything with memories, whether good or bad, as it can alter your emotions or distract from the process.

In this process, all five senses actively participate. From the preparation, your energy becomes more powerful than ever. Your senses must also be heightened, reaching an upgraded state. We will be using certain activators to achieve this.For smell, burn incense—I prefer bakhoor, as it has a strong influence and can resonate with the djinn. Whether you like the scent or not is irrelevant; its purpose is to trigger your sense of smell.

For hearing, play music without lyrics tuned to 432 Hz. It shouldn't be loud—just enough for you to hear. Place the device at a distance, like the other end of the room, but still within hearing range. The 432 Hz frequency is believed to attune your senses and facilitate connection with spiritual realms. It creates a calming, harmonious atmosphere, potentially enhancing your ability to hear them.

For touch, take two coins of any material. Place one in cold water or a refrigerator until it's cold, and the other should be warmed to a mild heat—something you can comfortably hold. Hold the cold coin in one hand and the warm coin in the other. The temperature contrast, while minimal and manageable, will help enhance your sense of touch during the process.

For taste, place a small pinch of salt in your mouth. Salt represents purity, preservation, and incorruptibility—qualities considered sacred. Its reverence comes from its life-sustaining properties, as it is a crucial element for human survival. Keep it minimal, don't overdo it. This small amount can boost and activate more than just your sense of taste.

For vision, you will sit in front of a mirror. You'll see your reflection, perhaps even more than that. One sight we can never experience directly is ourselves; we always need a reflection or copy to see our own image. In fact, the least observed thing in your life is you. By looking at yourself, you will activate and enhance your sense of vision.The first connection or presence will be sensed through one of the five senses. It doesn't matter which one, as the experience will manifest through at least one. Therefore, people with limitations in any of their senses will not face any issues during this process.

As I mentioned earlier, place the mirror on the front-facing wall. Natural light should enter from either the left or right side of the room, depending on your room's setup—it can be a window or any other opening. If the light enters from the right side, place a plant on the opposite side (the left). The plant must be alive; a desert plant is preferable, but any plant will work as long as it doesn't have flowers.The light opening doesn't need to be large, but at least a single ray of light must enter through it. This light should touch the mirror, the plant, and you. Ensure this happens and adjust the room setup accordingly.

Do not use a plant you already possess. It must come from outside, and you should collect it yourself by plucking it from the ground and placing it in a pot—don't buy it. The first touch on the plant must be yours. Before plucking, pour some water on it and ask permission, explaining to the plant what you are trying to achieve. After telling the plant your intentions, come back the next day. If the plant looks unwell, try another one. If the plant appears healthier than before, it has accepted your request, and you may pluck it.The plant serves as an energy carrier between your energy and the djinn's energy. Unlike other living things, plants exist with only positive energy and do not harbor any negative forces. This makes the plant an essential part of the process, which is why choosing the right one is crucial. That's also why you must seek its permission before taking it. Fortunately, 9 out of 10 times, the plant will accept.

On the back side of the room, place a stand with lights in seven colors, each corresponding to a chakra. The colors should be arranged from the base of the spine to the top of the head, reflecting the spectrum of a rainbow. The coloring order is:

1. Red - for the Root Chakra at the base of the spine

2. Orange - for the Sacral Chakra just below the navel

3. Yellow - for the Solar Plexus Chakra in the upper abdomen

4. Green - for the Heart Chakra in the center of the chest

5. Blue - for the Throat Chakra at the throat

6. Indigo - for the Third Eye Chakra on the forehead, between the eyes

7. Violet - for the Crown Chakra at the very top of the head.

It's important to set up the light source properly for this activity. Place colored lights in the order of the chakra colors behind you. When you sit in front of the mirror, make sure these lights shine on your back. You don't have to align the lights exactly with each chakra, but they should be in the right order. just make sure they are in the right order. Your chakras will pick up the energy from these lights on their own.We've talked about activating the senses, and these lights are meant to boost our energy and for the sixth sense. Our energy is pure and at its peak, but it's still contained within our own body. In the beginning, it's not easy to release this energy and reach out to external sources without the help of outside light, especially since our chakras are weak at this stage.You can set up a light stand with each color, which is the most effective way. If that's not possible, you can print or draw the colors in order and use a single light source to illuminate them. This will still allow you to follow the process.

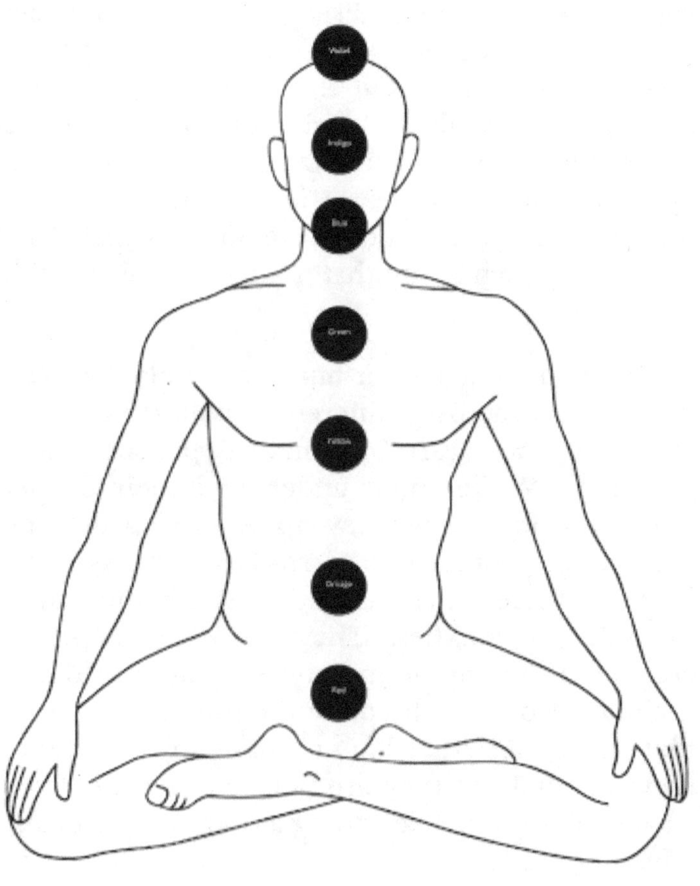
Violet
Indigo
Blue
Green
Orange
Red

On the ground, you're going to place the first symbol directly in front of you. It should be very close, positioned directly below your head. When you look down, you should see the symbol clearly and straight. On the ceiling, you'll place the second symbol. It should be positioned directly above your head so that when you look up, you can see it clearly and straight, just like the one on the ground. Make sure to place the symbols in such a way that it aligns perfectly with your view.

These are not just ordinary symbols. You can find them across different civilizations and religions, each carrying unique purposes and outcomes. While some understand their deeper meanings, for many, they appear to be nothing more than geometric patterns.Here, the symbols serve multiple functions, acting as a combination of different abilities. They work as a portal, creating an energy loop between your world and the outer world, with you in the middle to receive that energy. It's crucial not to make any changes to these symbols, as they are tantric in nature. Even a small alteration, like adding a dot, can drastically affect the outcome.

You can either draw these symbols or print them out. If needed, you can tear the page to use it, but make sure there are no alterations. Even a small change can affect the entire process. While you may come across similar symbols, don't let that mislead you. Be extremely cautious, as even a minute variation in the symbols can completely alter the results.The size of the symbols doesn't matter, but the most effective way to create them is on copper plates. However, this may not be practical for everyone. You can choose any method that works best for you—what matters is that both symbols are replicated exactly as they are, without any changes.

1.

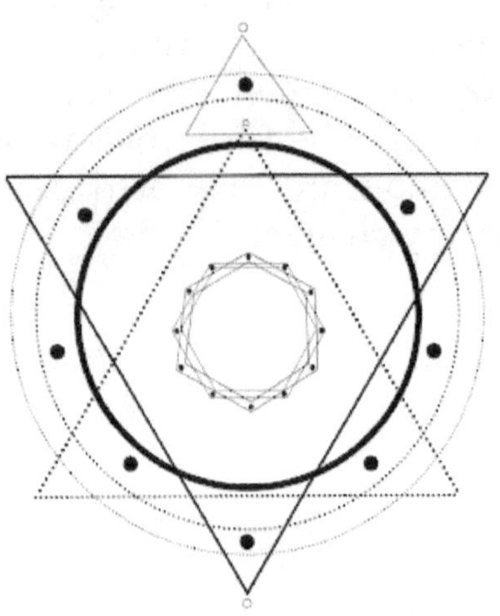

2.

Now you are going to place an energy storage device, which functions as a receiver, capturing outer energy. Throughout history, various storage devices have been used, the most notable being the Baghdad Battery. While its true purpose has been debated, I believe now you know the answer.Relax—you don't need to create a Baghdad battery. You can use a regular battery, Avoid using small clock batteries; I recommend using a small car battery instead. It's sufficient to store the necessary energy. The car battery will act as a stable and reliable energy storage unit, capable of holding a stronger charge, which will be more effective in capturing and channeling the energy required.but it must be completely dried out and without any charge. Remember, you are not storing electricity here. Place the battery on the opposite side of the plant, but not too close.

A white thread should be tied around the base of the plant's stem, just below the soil line. Make sure the end tied to the plant is buried under the soil. The other end of the thread should be tied to the first ring you used to wear. Ensure the thread is long enough to reach comfortably between the plant and the ring. A black thread should be tied securely to the battery, and the other end tied to the second ring you used to wear. Make sure the thread is long enough to connect both the battery and the ring without tension.

Place a bowl filled with water in front of you, between yourself and the mirror. Carefully place the two rings, which are tied to the threads (one from the plant and the other from the battery), into the water. The water used must be pure, free from impurities. The bowl can be made of any material, but it's recommended to use either a clay or copper bowl for optimal energy conduction.

The first part of the process is now complete. This setup may seem a bit complicated, but I've tried to simplify it as much as possible. When you consider the results you will achieve, it's worth the effort, so keep that in mind during times of fatigue. Trust the process.

CHAPTER 11

Connection

I'm glad you're here. Everything is set, and we've reached the final step of this journey. You've prepared yourself and the space with great care. Now let's get the connection. There is nothing to fear, and I know you're not feeling any. What you have within you now is not fear, but the drive—the fire—to conquer the unknown and to claim the rewards of your hard work and dedication. Embrace that energy and confidence as we take this final step. You're ready.

You need to wake up before 3 a.m.—you can't just stay up until that time. It's crucial that you sleep and then wake up from your rest. While some call it the "devil's hour," it's not just that; in many cultures, it's considered a sacred or auspicious time. In Hinduism, it's known as *Brahmamuhurta*, and in Islam, it's *Qiyam-u-lail*. This is the time when the veil between our world and other realms is at its thinnest, creating the perfect moment for connection. Many believe that prayers and intentions set during this time are more likely to be fulfilled, making it ideal for our purpose.

After waking up, get cleaned up by taking a bath. Drink some water, but don't eat anything. Move quickly through this process. Wear clothes without any stitching—clean, white-colored clothes are best. Make sure not to cover your back, as the lights need to shine directly on it. You can cover the rest of your body, but leave your back exposed for the lights.

After entering the room, follow the steps mentioned earlier to activate your senses. Perform this activation process for a few minutes, allowing your senses to fully awaken. Once your senses are activated, you can release the coins you've been holding. Now, remove your rings and tie them to the threads connected to the plant and battery. Drop the rings into the water-filled bowl in front of you.

The lights are shining on your chakras as you sit facing the mirror. Ensure you are in the Burmese position,Burmese is a seated meditation posture where you sit cross-legged with both feet resting on the floor, one in front of the other, without crossing them over each other. Your knees should touch the ground, and your back should be straight. You can choose to sit in either Burmese or Lotus position, depending on your comfort level.and your hands must be in Shakti Mudra.

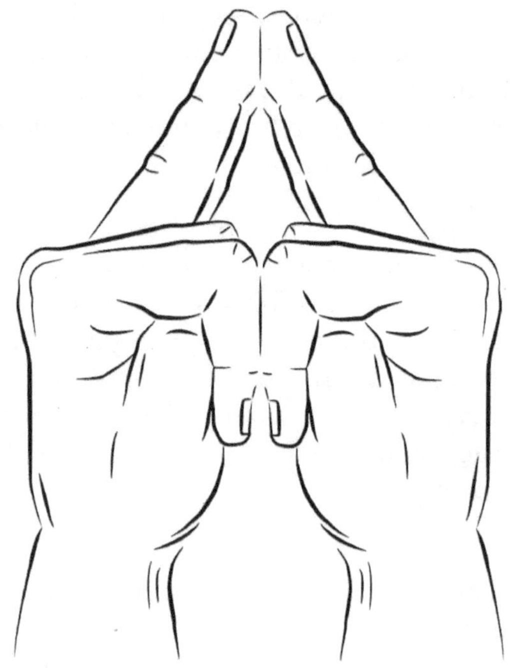

To form this mudra, tuck your thumbs into the center of your palms. Bend your index and middle fingers to lightly wrap around the thumbs, creating a secure hold. Extend your ring and little fingers outward, and then touch the tips of your ring and little fingers from both hands together.

Place the Shakti Mudra at the center of your chest and gently close your eyes. Begin to visualize the chakras and their corresponding colors glowing behind you, and imagine a steady flow of energy moving through your body. See the energy weaving through the tantric symbols, as though they are actively channeling power. Though your eyes are closed, this process is real—allow yourself to truly experience the flow of energy. Continue visualizing for some time, letting the connection deepen.

After some time, gently open your eyes and look into the mirror. Dip your hands into the water bowl in front of you, keeping them in the Shakti Mudra position. Return to your original position with the mudra held at the center of your chest. Repeat this process a total of 11 times—dipping your hands in the water and returning to position. Only open your eyes during the 1st and 11th time. The rest of the time, keep your eyes closed, staying focused on the energy flow and the process.Each time you dip your hands into the water and return to your position, try to feel the distant energy reaching out, attempting to connect with your own. Keep this thought clear in your mind throughout the process, focusing on the merging of your energy with the external force. Stay aware of the connection, and let yourself remain open to the flow of energy that is drawing closer with each movement.

After completing the process, relax your hands and gently lie down on the floor. Close your eyes and take a deep breath, holding it for a moment. At that instant, you may start to sense a presence. The early connection can come through any of your senses—sounds, smells, or even touch, like the sensation of a breeze gently brushing against you, though touch is quite rare. Taste might also occur, such as experiencing a sweet taste unexpectedly. However, vision doesn't usually happen this early in the process.In most cases, the first sign of connection with the djinn is through hearing subtle sounds.This is why activating your senses before starting the process is crucial. It helps to heighten your awareness and make you more receptive to the subtle energies and signals, whether they come through sound, smell, touch, or even taste. By preparing your senses, you increase your ability to detect and connect with these energies early on.

Be patient with this practice. You need to follow this routine for 40 days straight, and while you might not experience anything on the first day, the connection typically begins around day 5. although it varies from person to person. Patience and consistency are key to opening up to the energy . Stay consistent and don't rush the results.This process can sometimes extend beyond 40 days, but you will experience signals and improvements every day. These daily signs of progress will keep you motivated, so you won't feel discouraged during the journey. Just stay patient and consistent, and the results will come in time.

When you start to feel the presence of the djinn through your senses, it's natural to feel a bit scared at first. However, the djinn want to connect with you as an ally, not to cause harm. Remember, they are drawn to strength and courage. They don't seek connection with the weak or fearful. So, stay confident and know that you are in control.you are not afraid of them.

It some point, you will begin to hear sounds from the djinn. It can happen on any day of your practice. As you continue to progress, those sounds will evolve into voices, as if they are speaking directly to you. This marks a significant stage in the process and is one of the key signs of progress.Once you reach this stage, the rest will unfold quickly, leading to a complete connection between you and the djinn. At that point, the bond will be stronger from that point, and everything will fall into place naturally and you will start seeing them in the mirror, though at first, it won't be very clear. Initially, you'll only perceive a reflection of their energy rather than a distinct image. But as the days progress, the image will become clearer and clearer. Seeing them directly with your eyes, beyond just their reflection, will only happen at the very end of the process.

Like I mentioned earlier, if the connection happens and you start conversing with the djinn, but they ask for something in return, it's a sign that this is not the djinn you are seeking. Reject the connection immediately. If you choose not to respond or ignore their requests, it won't bother you or cause any harm. The key is to remain calm and confident in your intention. By not engaging with these requests, you maintain control over the situation. Keep focusing on your process, Continue with your practice as instructed and the real connection will come to you soon.

The entire process should conclude before sunrise, ideally lasting no more than 40 minutes. Once you finish, put the rings back on your fingers and go about your day, wearing them as usual. Repeat this process daily until the connection is fully established.

Soon, you'll have a full connection with the djinn, where you can see and communicate with them directly. You'll be surprised by how happy the djinn will be for this connection—they've been waiting for this moment even more than you. Once the connection is complete, the djinn will guide you further. You can ask for your desires, your needs, and anything you wish for. At this point, you will have achieved a full connection—you've won the djinn.

You don't need me anymore. You've already won your first djinn and can now act according to the guidance it provides. When you do, ask the djinn about *The club*. The djinn will reveal it to you—there are others like you in that club. When you're ready, we'll meet there.

I'm waiting for you.

www.ingramcontent.com/pod-product-compliance
Lightning Source LLC
LaVergne TN
LVHW041114150826
845673LV00007B/2043

9798896101765